# Stewie
## The Eagle

DANE STEWART

ISBN:   Softcover        978-1-7960-3774-6
        EBook            978-1-7960-3775-3

Print information available on the last page

Rev. date: 05/31/2019

To order additional copies of this book, contact:
Xlibris
1-888-795-4274
www.Xlibris.com
Orders@Xlibris.com

# STEWIE THE EAGLE

## Written By;

## Dane A, Stewart

# THANKS

To my dear friend and colleague Joan Webb for her ideas. To my sister Melanie McKitty Martin and my brother Anthony Stewart for their moral support. To Ryza Jones my publishing consultant.

Stewie the unique eagle is a type of bird that is called a "bird of prey". He is an expert flier, and is known for his excellent hunting abilities.

I dedicate this book to Danea Natasha Stewart, my daughter who inspired me to write this extraordinary book.

For years people have seen Stewie as an icon of beauty, bravery, courage, honor, pride, determination, and grace. This bird is important and symbolic to humanity because of its characteristics.

ADVENTUROUS

ADAPTABLE

INTELLIGENT

COURAGEOUS

AMBITIOUS

HUMBLE

HAPPY

SKILFULL

COMPASSIONATE

VISSIONAIRE

Stewie is known for his weighty head and curved beak. He is also known for his strong, muscular legs and sharp, powerful talons. He has a spacious wingspan and is covered in multicolored feathers which provides insulation, and protection from the environment.

Stewie builds his nest in large trees on the peak of mountains or near rivers or coasts. He often extends and uses the same nest year after year. His nest is so

**enormous**, as much as 9 feet in diameter, weighing two tons.

Even birds need to **play** at some pointing time. Stewie sometimes toss or pass sticks to other eagles in the air.

FLY

FLIP

Flop

FLOP

FLIP

FLY

Stewie tries not to LAUGH! LAUGH! LAUGH! at his own jokes, But we all

know he's **hilarious.**

Stewie flies alone at high altitude and not with sparrows or with other small birds. No other bird can go to the height that Stewie goes

CIRCLE          CIRCUMNAVIGATE

                FLOAT
MANEUVER
                MOUNT

"I'm going to

FLY            FLY            FLY

HIGH           HIGH           HIGH


ACROSS THE


SKY            SKY            SKY

and view the landmasses and water
bodies of the world."

# Why do Stewie Fly So High?

Whenever Stewie is flying high and screaming he is in fact claiming the respective land, admonition other predators to stay away. From the heights of the sky, Stewie easily finds rivers, forests and other hunting areas, being able to get down on the ground

with an **incredible** speed.

DASH                    SWOOP

DIVE        WHIZ        RUSH


SHOOT                   LIGHTENING-BOLT

            HURRY

    JET


ZOOM                    ROCKET


                        WHOOSH

Stewie's high-flying lifestyle requires super strong vision. He has the ability to focus on something up to two miles away. When Stewie sites his prey, it becomes his center of attraction. He narrows his focus on it and sets out to get it. No matter the difficulty, Stewie will not move his focus from the prey until he grabs it

Stewie's BIG FOCUS VISION PRODUCES BIG RESULTS.

LOOK INTO IT

LOOK OVER IT

LOOK ABOVE IT

LOOK AT IT

LOOK FORWARD

LOOD BEYOND IT

Do you see what you need?

ITS YOURS!!!

Stewie loves the storm. When massive gray-black clouds congregate, he gets very **excited**. He uses the storm's boisterous winds to ELEVATE him.

Once Stewie finds the wing of the storm, he uses the raging storm to lift him above the thick dark clouds. This gives him a wonderful opportunity to glide and take it easy as he relaxes his wings. In the meantime all the other birds hide in the dense leaves and dwarf branches of the trees.

When Stewie got older, his feathers became very weak and could not take him as fast as it should. When he feels extremely weak and about to give up, he retires to a place far away in the cleft of the rocks.

While there, he loses every beautiful feather BIT BY BIT, ONE BY ONE. He stays in this quiet place of refuge until he has grown new VIBRANT feathers, then he comes out and ......

# soar     soar

# soar

as an

# ambassador!!!

CPSIA information can be obtained
at www.ICGtesting.com
Printed in the USA
BVHW021204060619
550349BV00003B/29/P